Santa meets the Headless Horseman

A Children's Book for Adults

Written and Illustrated by

Alyssa and Lee Ehrlich

© 2018 by Haunted Road Media.
All rights reserved. No part of this book may be reproduced, stored in a retrieval system or transmitted in any form or by any means without the prior written permission of the publishers, except by a reviewer who may quote brief passages in a review to be printed in a newspaper, magazine or journal.

PUBLISHED BY HAUNTED ROAD MEDIA, LLC
www.hauntedroadmedia.com

United States of America

HO HO HO...

HO HO HO...

O HO HO...

HO HO HO...

HO HO...

About the Authors

Alyssa Ehrlich is a photographer and explorer with a penchant for urban exploration. Her interests have taken her around the world, and she is equally at home searching for ancient relics, as she is discovering the wonders of the paranormal.

Lee Ehrlich is an Adventurer/Explorer most who is most notably recognized as the World Authority on Underwater Paranormal Phenomena. He is a Paranormal Investigator with over three decades of experience, who heads a nation-wide investigative team specializing in hostile and dangerous environments. His investigative exploits have earned him critical acclaim, which has resulted in numerous radio and television appearances, including a starring role in The Travel Channel's "Legends Of." On the conference tour, he is a well-known lecturer, who brings a unique perspective to the paranormal realm.

www.ingramcontent.com/pod-product-compliance
Lightning Source LLC
Chambersburg PA
CBHW041008170626
46815CB00002B/212